W9-CYT-738

A Bale of Turtles

Lee Clancey and Mary Rothermel

Archway Publishing books may be ordered through booksellers or by contacting:

Archway Publishing
1663 Liberty Drive
Bloomington, IN 47403
www.archwaypublishing.com
1 (888) 242-5904

ISBN: 978-1-4808-2046-3 (sc)
ISBN: 978-1-4808-2047-0 (hc)
ISBN: 978-1-4808-2045-6 (e)

Print information available on the last page.

Archway Publishing rev. date: 08/18/2015

This book is dedicated from Mooshie to the "littles" of her CLAN, Lulu and Wilson, with lots of love!

INTRODUCTION:

In the animal world, each animal has its own name, but there are also names for groups of the same kind of animal. For example, when more than one monkey gather together, the group of monkeys is called a troop. The naming of animal groups began a long time ago, in the 1400s, as hunters named groups of animals and birds that they hunted.

Did you know that ...

One little turtle is only a turtle

But more than one is a bale?

Whales in a family are called a POD
But friends are a GAM of whales.

A lone jellyfish floats in the sea
And she is soon joined by a smack.

A SCHOOL of dolphins swims nearby,
They already have their pack.

There is a LITTER of puppies, a
KINDLE of kittens,
And even a CLOWDER of cats!

And deep in caves flying sonar at night
Is a squeaking **colony** of bats.

A **peep** of chickens and a clutch of eggs
You'll find in nests in the coop.

A gaggle of geese, a rafter of turkeys,
A paddling of ducks makes each group.

While on the farm live a TRIP of goats,
A DRIFT of hogs and cattle in a DROVE.

And in the fields graze a flock of sheep
With strings of ponies on the rove.

Deep in the ground dwells a labor of moles
Sharing space with a rabbit nest.

Directly above creeps an ARMY of caterpillars
And giant ant COLONIES never at rest.

High up in the sky a **tidings** of magpies
And a **richness** of ravens soar.

But out in the woods a **sloth** of bears
Runs the forest floor.

A skulk of fancy foxes
Resides in the forest, too.

Along with a serious business of ferrets
These names are all quite true!

A parliament of owls hoot, hoot while flying on a breeze.
And a descent of woodpeckers taps and drums on all the nearby trees.

The names of animal groups

Are funny and alive.

Just like a swarm of busy bees

In a bustling, buzzing hive!

CPSIA information can be obtained at www.ICGtesting.com
Printed in the USA
LVOW02*0348120915

453847LV00009BA/64/P